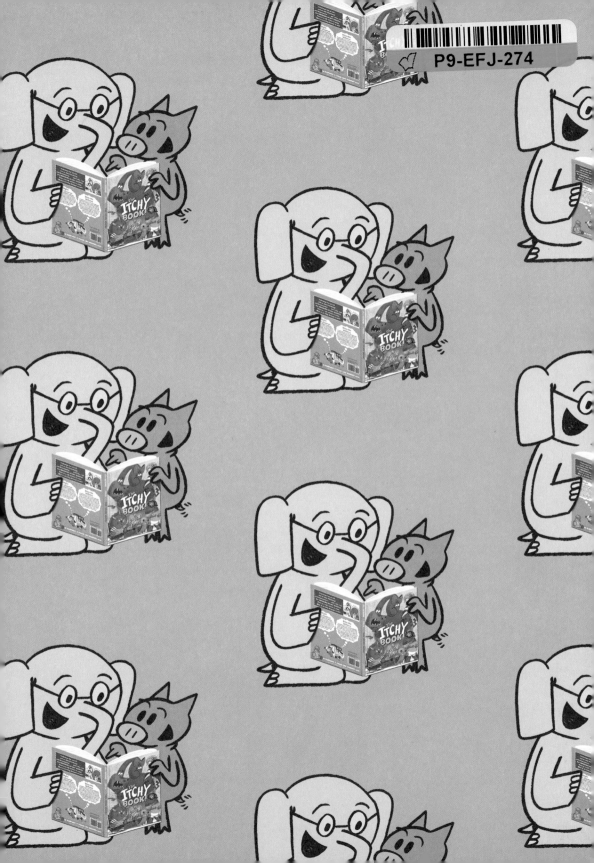

I *feel* you will love it!

MO WILLEMS'
ELEPHANT & PIGGIE
LIKE READING!

The ITCHY BOOK!

BY LeUyEN PHAM

An **ELEPHANT & PIGGIE LIKE READING!** Book

Hyperion Books for Children / *New York*

AN IMPRINT OF DISNEY BOOK GROUP

To Dino-Mo and Tracey-teratops
—L.P.

"Dinosaurs do not scratch."

Who knew?

9

BZZZZ

STOP!

WHAT are you doing?!

I have an itch.
I want to scratch it.

Read the sign!

"Dinosaurs
do not scratch."

Are you a dinosaur or not?

Of course I am a dinosaur! Who said I am not a dinosaur? Some BIRD?!

Look! She has an itch too. She is a TOUGH DINOSAUR.

BUT IT IS SUPER ITCHY DOWN THERE!

Hey, guys. What are you doing?

We are being tough dinosaurs. What's up?

Grrr...

Ermm...

15

My back is itchy.
Would one of you tough
dinosaurs scratch
it for me, please?

25

26

You tell him.

35

Wow, did that feel GOOD!

I cannot believe we waited so long!

The sign was right.

We really are TOUGH DINOSAURS!

I wonder why dinosaurs do not scratch alone?

Uh . . .

49

First Edition, May 2018 • 1 3 5 7 9 10 8 6 4 2 • FAC-034274-18089 • Printed in the United States of America
This book is set in Century 725/Monotype; Grilled Cheese BTN/Fontbros, with hand-lettering by LeUyen Pham
Library of Congress Cataloging-in-Publication Data
Names: Willems, Mo, author, illustrator. | Pham, LeUyen, author, illustrator. | Title: The itchy book! / by [Mo Willems and] LeUyen Pham. | Description: First edition. | Los Angeles ; New York : Hyperion Books for Children, an imprint of Disney Book Group, [2018] | Series: Elephant & Piggie like reading! | Summary: Triceratops, Pterodactyl, Brontosaurus, and T-Rex each have an itch, but Dino-Mo reminds them of the sign with a very important rule: Dinosaurs do not scratch. Identifiers: LCCN 2017046405 | ISBN 9781368005647 (hardback) | Subjects: | CYAC: Itching—Fiction. Dinosaurs—Fiction. | Humorous stories. | BISAC: JUVENILE FICTION / Animals / Dinosaurs & Prehistoric Creatures. JUVENILE FICTION / Social Issues / General (see also headings under Family). | JUVENILE FICTION / Humorous Stories. | Classification: LCC PZ7.W65535 Ism 2018 | DDC [E]—dc23 | LC record available at https://lccn.loc.gov/2017046405
Reinforced binding
Visit hyperionbooksforchildren.com and pigeonpresents.com

**Elephant & Piggie
also like reading:**

The Cookie Fiasco
by Dan Santat

We Are Growing!
by Laurie Keller
(Theodor Seuss Geisel Medal)

The Good for Nothing Button!
by Charise Mericle Harper

It's Shoe Time!
by Bryan Collier